Katie Woo

Katie Blows Her Top

by Fran Manushkin

illustrated by Tammie Lyon

raintree

a Capstone company — publishers for children

Raintree is an imprint of Capstone Global Library Limited, a company incorporated in England and Wales having its registered office at 264 Banbury Road, Oxford, OX2 7DY – Registered company number: 6695582

www.raintree.co.uk
myorders@raintree.co.uk

Graphic Designer: Ted Williams
Printed and bound in India

ISBN 978 1 4747 8224 1
23 22 21 20 19
10 9 8 7 6 5 4 3 2 1

British Library Cataloguing in Publication Data
A full catalogue record for this book is available from the British Library.

Acknowledgements
Fran Manushkin, pg. 26
Tammie Lyon, pg. 26

Contents

Chapter 1
A blast at school.................................5

Chapter 2
What a mess!..............................13

Chapter 3
KABOOM!.............................21

Chapter 1
A blast at school

Katie was feeling tip-top.

She told her dad, "Today

I'm going to learn about

volcanoes. It will be a blast!"

On the way to school,

Pedro said, "Volcanoes are

awesome! But I don't want

to be near one."

"I do," said Katie. "I want

to hear the KABOOM!"

Miss Winkle told the class, "When hot melted rock and gas reach the top of the mountain – BOOM! The volcano explodes. It can bury a city."

"Sometimes we know

when a volcano blast is

coming," said Miss Winkle.

"Sometimes it's a surprise."

"I have a surprise for you," said Miss Winkle. "Today we are making volcanoes! We will work in teams."

Katie picked JoJo and Pedro.

Miss Winkle gave them some clay and a bottle.

She said, "The first step is to mould this clay around the bottle. Try to make the shape of a mountain."

Pedro grabbed all the clay

and tried to make a mountain.

"Stop!" said Katie. "Our

mountain is lumpy!"

"Lumpy is fun," Pedro said.

"No!" said Katie. "Lumpy

is wrong!"

"The clay will need

time to dry," said Miss

Winkle. "We will finish our

volcanoes after lunch."

Chapter 2
What a mess!

At lunchtime, Katie told

Pedro, "Don't be a volcano

hog. I want to do the rest! I

know I can make it explode."

"Hey!" yelled JoJo. "What

about me?"

After lunch, Miss Winkle

gave each team white vinegar

and red food colouring to mix

in a bowl.

"Let's make the lava super-red," said Katie.

Oops! She poured in too much, and the red spilled on her T-shirt.

"Yuck!"

Katie groaned.

"What a mess!"

"The next step," said Miss

Winkle, "is to pour baking

soda onto a paper towel."

"I'll do it," said Pedro.

"No. Me!" said JoJo.

JoJo tried to grab the baking soda. Oops! The soda went flying and landed on Katie's head!

"Yikes!" yelled JoJo. "You are a mess!"

KABOOM!

That's when Katie blew her top. Her cheeks got hot and red, and she made angry faces.

"Wow!" said Pedro.

"You are fierce! You said

you wanted to be close to

a volcano. And you are!

You've become a volcano!"

"I am a volcano?" said Katie. "Wow! Sometimes I *am* a bit fierce."

"Yes, you are," agreed Miss Winkle. She sent Katie to clean herself up.

Later, JoJo told Katie,

"Let's start a new volcano,

and this time we will be fair.

We will each do our share."

Katie did the last step: she poured the baking soda into the bottle.

When it mixed with the vinegar –

KABOOM!

The lava poured out.

"Wow!" shouted everyone.

"Amazing!"

"High five!" said Katie,

Pedro and JoJo.

After school, Katie said, "Let's be volcanoes all the way home."

"Kaboom!"

"Kaboom!"

"KABOOOOOM!"

About the author

Fran Manushkin is the author of many popular picture books, including *Baby, Come Out!*; *Latkes and Applesauce: A Hanukkah Story*; *The Belly Book* and *Big Girl Panties*. There is a real Katie Woo – she's Fran's great-niece – but she never gets in half the trouble that Katie Woo does in the books. Fran writes on her beloved Mac computer in New York City, USA, without the help of her two naughty cats, Chaim and Goldy.

About the illustrator

Tammie Lyon began her love for drawing at a young age while sitting at the kitchen table with her dad. She continued her love of art and eventually attended college, where she earned a bachelor's degree in fine art. After a brief career as a professional ballet dancer, she decided to devote herself full-time to illustration. Today she lives with her husband, Lee, in Cincinnati, Ohio, USA. Her dogs, Gus and Dudley, keep her company as she works in her studio.

Glossary

baking soda a white powder used in baking to make dough rise

clay a kind of earth that can be shaped when wet

explode blow apart with a loud bang and great force

fierce daring and dangerous or strong

gas something that is not liquid or solid and does not have a definite shape

lava the hot, liquid rock that pours out of a volcano when it erupts

melted changed from a solid to a liquid

vinegar a sour liquid that is used to flavour food

volcano a mountain with openings through which lava, ash and gas may erupt

Let's talk

1. Katie picked her friends to be on her team. Is that a good way to pick teams? Why or why not? How do you pick teams?

2. Pedro compared Katie to a volcano. How is Katie like a volcano?

3. Katie's team started again with a new volcano. Compare the second time they built a volcano to the first. What did Katie and her team do differently?

Let's write

1. Research volcanoes and write a paragraph about what you learned.

2. List the things about Katie's volcano project that made her angry. Then make a list of some times when you have been angry. What made you feel better?

3. Miss Winkle taught the teams each step to make their volcanoes. Using the book as your guide, write down the steps you would need to do to make a volcano. Pretend you are writing these instructions to a friend.

Having fun with Katie Woo!

Katie Woo and her friends built a volcano. They had a blast! Now you can build your own volcano too. Get your friends together to help. Just be sure to share the work!

Exploding volcano

What you need:

- a big bin bag
- scissors
- an empty plastic water bottle
- a funnel
- air-dry clay
- an old bowl
- 1 cup of white vinegar
- red food colouring
- 4 tablespoons of baking soda
- a paper towel

What you do:

1. Cut open the bin bag, and spread it out to protect your work surface.

2. Mould the clay around the bottle in a cone shape. Make sure the top of the cone is a little taller than the top of the bottle. Let the clay dry for at least one hour.

3. Pour the vinegar into the old bowl. Add 5 or 6 drops of red food colouring to the vinegar for red "lava."

4. Put the funnel in the top of the plastic bottle inside your volcano. Carefully pour the coloured vinegar into the bottle through the funnel.

5. Pour the baking soda onto the paper towel. Then, using the funnel, pour the baking soda from the towel into the vinegar in the plastic bottle.

6. Stand back and watch your volcano explode!